Boom . . . Boom . . . Boom . . .

DINOSAUR WEEKLY

horrible horns

gigantic jaws

evil eyes

scaly skin

Boom . . . Boom . . . Boo

"Well, I've heard he's got six hundred **razor sharp** teeth!" said Serra.

Boom . . . Boom .

"You mean to say YOU'RE the fiercest, meanest, scariest dinosaur ever to walk the earth?" asked Stegg.

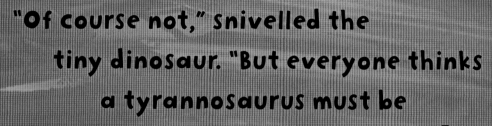

"Of course not," snivelled the
tiny dinosaur. "But everyone thinks
a tyrannosaurus must be

ugly and **Nasty**

so they run away when
they see me and my
brother coming."

sniff!